The Perfect Hug

To Isaac and Freya,
wishing them many hugs
– *JW*

A chi mi stringe da sempre
nell'abbraccio perfetto,
papà Pino e mamma Rita!
– *JA*

SIMON AND SCHUSTER
First published in Great Britain in 2011 by Simon and Schuster UK Ltd
1st Floor, 222 Gray's Inn Road, London WC1X 8HB
A CBS Company

Text copyright © 2011 Joanna Walsh
Illustrations copyright © 2011 Giuditta Gaviraghi

ISBN: 978-1-84738-591-8 (HB)
ISBN: 978-1-84738-592-5 (PB)
Printed in Italy
4 6 8 10 9 7 5 3

The Perfect Hug

Joanna Walsh & Judi Abbot

SIMON AND SCHUSTER
London   New York   Sydney

There are **hugs** for wrigglers,

and **hugs** for gigglers.

Hugs that are tickly,

and **hugs** that are prickly . . .

But none is exactly the right **hug** for me!

I'm out to find the perfect kind.

How big is a **hug**?

A bug may mean well,
but how can I feel his tiny squeeze
around my knees?

A boa constrictor's **hug's** a bit STRICTER than any sort of **hug** ought to be (at least for me)!

A **hug** from a grizzly
is big but scary.

Grin and bear it,
but do be wary.

Then there's the question of arms.
What's too many?

Some have lots.

And some not any!

And what about a jellyfish,
with all those stingers?

I'd **hug** her with rubber gloves on my fingers.

None of these **hugs** is quite the height for,
not too tight for, oh-so-right for me.
But . . .

Could there be **hugs** light years from here?
Hugs we know nothing about,

far out, on stars in a galaxy far, far away?
How DO they **hug** the Milky Way way?

I've tried them all,

short and TALL

BIG

and small.

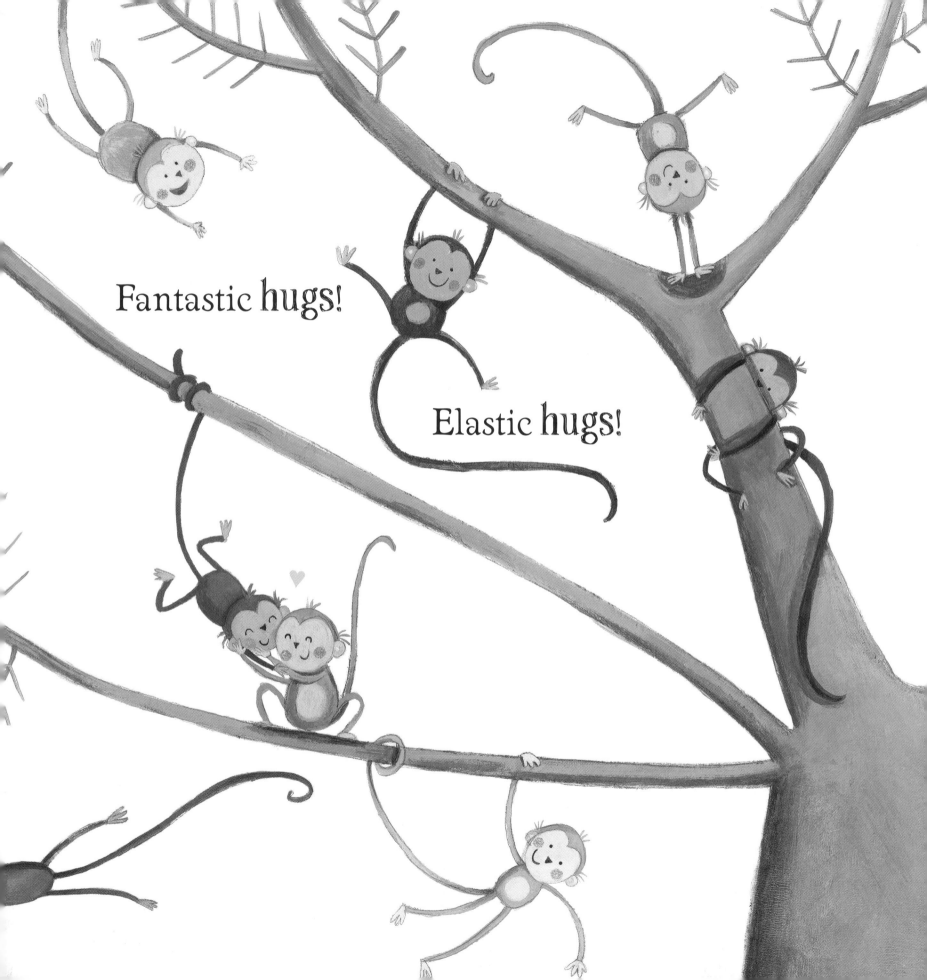

Fantastic hugs!

Elastic hugs!

Gymnastic,
enthusiastic hugs!
But . . .

Where will I find one that's just my size?

One that will suit me down to the ground?
One that will fit me all the way round?

I've roved the wide seas, over and under, and still I wonder . . .

Do you suppose,
    there might be a hug right under my nose?

            What's the secret?
            "Tell!"

"Well . . .
It's easy peasy.
Don't you know?
It's one plus one.
A hug takes two."

PERFECT HUG

If you hug me,
then I'll hug you!